THE POWERPUFF GIRLS

MOVIE

A Novelization

Adapted from the script by Charlie Bean, Lauren Faust, Craig McCracken,
Amy Keating Rogers, Paul Rudish, and Don Shank
Based on "THE POWERPUFF GIRLS," as created by Craig McCracken

SCHOLASTIC INC.

New York   Toronto   London   Auckland   Sydney
Mexico City   New Delhi   Hong Kong   Buenos Aires

No part of this publication may be reproduced in whole or in part, or stored in a retrieval system, or transmitted in any form or by any means, electronic, mechanical, photocopying, recording, or otherwise, without written permission of the publisher. For information regarding permission, write to Scholastic Inc., Attention: Permissions Department, 557 Broadway, New York, NY 10012.

ISBN 0-439-38127-4

Copyright © 2002 by Cartoon Network.
CARTOON NETWORK, the logo, THE POWERPUFF GIRLS, and all related characters and elements are trademarks of and © Cartoon Network.
(s02)
Published by Scholastic Inc. All rights reserved.
SCHOLASTIC and associated logos are trademarks and/or registered trademarks of Scholastic Inc.

Interior illustrations by the Thompson Brothers.

Designed by Peter Koblish

12 11 10 9 8 7 6 5 4 3 2 1   2 3 4 5 6 7/0

Printed in the U.S.A.
First Scholastic printing, July 2002

chapter 1

The city of Townsville . . . was once a town so vile, so dark, so infested with evil that its inhabitants called it the "city of Townsvillainy."

Robbers raged and ran rampant. Criminals carried out callous cruelty. Monsters made major messes.

But worst of all, the citizens of Townsville had lost their most valuable of all possessions . . . hope.

Still, one man, a lone scientist in his basement laboratory, was working on an experiment that *could make life sweet again, that would spice up the citizens' lives and make everything nice.*

It was late at night. As usual, the Professor's monkey lab assistant, Jojo, was goofing around mischievously, breaking everything in sight. But the Professor was working too hard to pay much attention to little Jojo. He gathered together the ingredients for his newest creation. Concentrating, he poured the ingredients into a pot.

"Hmmm . . ." the Professor said. "The perfect little girl. Sugar, spice . . . and a nice big helping of everything nice."

But as the Professor was mixing his concoction, Jojo ran up to him and pushed him. The Professor stumbled and crashed into a beaker on a nearby shelf. The beaker was labeled CHEMICAL X.

The Professor watched in horror as the liquid from the beaker poured into his mixture. The concoction in the pot began to boil and bubble.

The Professor backed slowly away. He knew that Chemical X was very, very powerful. There was no telling what would happen. But the impish Jojo stayed behind, peeking into the bubbling brew.

Suddenly — *KABOOM*! There was a tremendous explosion. The Professor was knocked unconscious against a wall.

When he came to, he opened his eyes and stared in shock. His jaw dropped in utter amazement at what he saw.

Standing in front of the pot were not one, but *three* perfect little girls — a redhead, a blond, and a brunet. The Professor was stunned.

"Hi, what's your name?" the redhead asked in a friendly voice.

The Professor jumped back in astonishment. Then he pulled himself together. "Oh . . . my name is, uh, Professor! Professor Utonium."

"Hello, Professor Utonium," the three girls said together. "It's very nice to meet you."

3

"It's nice to meet you, too," the Professor said. "Um, uh . . . what are your names?"

"Well, you made us," the redhead said. "Shouldn't *you* name us?"

"Oh, right," the Professor said. "Let's see." He looked at the redhead. "Well, you're so direct, and you opened right up to me. I think I'll call you . . . Blossom."

Blossom smiled.

The blond began to giggle. The Professor turned to her. "And you're so cute and bubbly. I think I'll call you Bubbles."

Bubbles smiled.

The Professor turned to the brunet. She smiled at him eagerly. "So, let's see. We have Blossom, Bubbles, and uh . . . Buttercup! Because that begins with a *B*, too!"

Buttercup scowled. Her name didn't have a cool meaning like her sisters' did.

"I can't believe it!" the Professor said happily. "Just what I wanted! To make some kids, who I could teach right from wrong, good from bad! And I hope in turn that maybe they'd do some good for this terrible town!" The Professor was beaming. "Sugar and spice and everything nice! Who would have guessed that that's actually what little girls are made of! I can't believe it worked!" The Professor raced up the stairs of his laboratory. He was so happy, he wanted to get gifts for the girls. "I actually made three perfect little girls, three normal little g — aaaah!"

The Professor tripped on a step. He flew through the air. But just as he was about to land on the ground with a thud, something stopped him. The Professor looked down and saw Blossom holding him in midair. She floated down and rested him safely on the ground.

"You should be more careful, Professor," she said. "You could get hurt."

Bubbles and Buttercup zoomed through the air and landed next to them.

The Professor stared at his three girls in amazement. Then he looked over at the pot he had used to mix up the potion. The container of Chemical X was still dripping into the pot. He smiled. Maybe Chemical X wasn't such a bad ingredient after all!

But wait! Who's that in the corner, Professor? Your little girls may be wonderful creations, but you're overlooking something else your Chemical X did. It looks like Jojo was caught in the Chemical X blast, too! And look what it did to him!

Lurking in the corner of the lab, watching the Professor and the girls with resentment, was Jojo. But he wasn't the same prankish little lab monkey he had been before. His skin had turned a sickly green, and his brain was beginning to swell to an enormous size.

And that's not all! Look at the nasty gleam in his eye! Better watch out, girls — that Jojo looks like he has a bad case of simian rivalry!

chapter 2

The next day!

The Professor stood in the girls' new room. He held a roller with paint on it. Blossom, Bubbles, and Buttercup all had paint rollers, too.

"Okay, girls, now watch me," the Professor said.

But even before he could start to show them, the girls began whizzing around the room at superspeed. In a flash, they had painted the whole room — and the Professor, too!

The Professor laughed, looking down at the pink paint that covered him. "Okay, I guess I'll go wash up. Then we'll bring in the furniture."

But when the Professor walked out of the bathroom, he saw furniture flying up the stairs into the girls' room.

"Girls, wait!" the Professor called. "That stuff's heavy! You should let me . . . help. . . ." But it was too late. When the Professor walked into the girls' room, everything was set up — a dresser, a night table, and a nice big bed. "Wow! This looks pretty good."

"It's a little bit dark," Bubbles said.

"Well, I like it dark," Buttercup grumbled.

"Some windows might be nice," Blossom suggested.

The Professor nodded. "Yeah, I could see some windows right about here. I'll call a contractor tomor —" He stopped abruptly. While he was talking, Blossom, Bubbles, and Buttercup had turned and focused on the wall. Three sets of laser beams shot out of their eyes and cut three perfect oval windows in the wall.

"Well, that works, doesn't it?" the stunned Professor said with a smile.

The next day at Pokey Oaks Kindergarten, that hallowed hall of scholarship and knowledge . . . not to mention finger paints, rest time, and snacks!

A nice woman stood at the door to the school. "Hello, girls," she said brightly. "I'm your teacher, Ms. Keane. Welcome to our school."

"What's a school?" Blossom asked.

Ms. Keane smiled kindly. "It's where kids come to learn."

The girls looked around. They saw lots of other children playing, sitting at desks, reading, doing crafts, and having fun.

A boy walked up to the girls. "Hey, wanna play?" he asked.

"Sure!" The girls ran off to join the fun.

The Professor stood with Ms. Keane. "Do

you think they'll be okay?" he asked. "Because I'm new at this parenting thing. And they're really special. I mean *really* special."

"They'll be just fine," Ms. Keane said with a smile. "We'll see you at dismissal time."

"Okay," the Professor replied. "Bye, girls! Bye! Bye! Have a good day! Bye-bye!" He hung back, still nervous about leaving.

Finally, Ms. Keane gently pushed him out the door and shut it behind him. She turned to the children. "Okay, class, take your seats."

"Ms. Keane!" a girl called out. "Can Blossom sit with us?"

Another girl piped up. "Can we sit with Bubbles?"

"Can Buttercup sit over here?" a boy asked. He was wearing a T-shirt that said MITCH ROCKS.

"The girls can sit right here," Ms. Keane told the class. "In the middle, so they'll be next to everyone."

"Yaaay!" the kids cheered.

The three little girls had a great day

at school. Bubbles made a pretty picture. Buttercup built a tower of blocks and knocked it down. Blossom taught herself to read, add, subtract, multiply, and divide. Before the girls knew it, it was time for dismissal.

"Boys and girls, you can play in the school yard while you wait for your parents," Ms. Keane announced.

The Professor arrived at twelve o'clock on the dot. The classroom was very untidy — toys and books were everywhere.

"Did everything go all right?" he asked, surveying the messy scene.

"Just great," Ms. Keane said with a smile.

"Nothing happened?" the Professor said. "Nothing . . . out of the ordinary?"

"Your girls were just perfect normal little girls," Ms. Keane assured him.

The Professor sighed happily. He looked out over the school yard. His little girls were standing with a group of children, watching the other kids play.

Just then, Mitch tagged a little girl playing hopscotch. "Tag! You're it!" he cried. The little girl squealed and ran away. And all the other kids ran away from *her*.

"Whoa, everyone's running from that girl. It's like she's infected," Blossom said.

"Maybe she's a freak," Buttercup added.

"Yeah, and they hate her," Bubbles said.

Then the little girl ran up and tagged Bubbles. "Tag! You're It!" she yelled.

"Oh, no, I've been affected!" Bubbles cried. She took a step forward. As soon as she did, all the other children shrieked and ran away.

Bubbles's eyes filled with tears. "Everybody hates me!"

Mitch shook his head in amazement. "No, they don't! It's just a game."

"It is?" Bubbles said.

"A game! Neat!" Blossom said.

"How do we play?" Buttercup asked.

"It's simple," Mitch explained. "When you're

tagged, you're It. All you have to do is tag someone else. Go ahead, Bubbles, tag someone!"

Bubbles turned to Buttercup and tagged her. She giggled. "You're It!"

"Tag someone, Buttercup!" Mitch said.

Buttercup looked at her sisters.

"Oh, no you don't!" Blossom said, running away.

Bubbles giggled and followed her sister.

Buttercup raced after them.

"Uh-oh, here she comes! Time to put it into overdrive, Bubbles!" Blossom called.

Blossom and Bubbles sped up. Buttercup did, too. Soon Buttercup started *flying* full force, trying to catch up with her sisters. They started flying, too, trying to get away from her.

Buttercup zoomed through the air so fast that a green flare formed behind her. The flare grew brighter as Buttercup flew faster. Finally, it exploded with a loud *BANG*! Buttercup streaked through the school yard, setting portions of the ground on fire as she went.

Then Buttercup really turned up the speed. She was gaining fast on Bubbles. She tagged her sister as hard as she could. "Tag! You're It!"

The force of the tag thrust Bubbles backward. She tore up the concrete of the playground as she plowed across it. Finally, Bubbles smashed through the wall of the school, sending bricks flying everywhere.

Meanwhile, the rest of the kids were frightened and confused. They didn't understand what was happening. Ms. Keane rounded them up and headed for cover. The Professor stood rooted in his spot, staring in astonishment.

A moment later, Bubbles blasted out the roof of the school, a huge smile on her face.

"I'm going to tag you guys now!" Bubbles called to her sisters.

She zoomed toward them. They sped up, trying to get away. Bubbles was gaining on them. But just as she was about to reach them,

Blossom and Buttercup changed direction. Bubbles crashed into the ground, creating a huge crater around her when she landed.

"Ha-ha! You missed us!" Buttercup teased.

Bubbles flew out of the crater. She spotted her sisters outside the school yard, by a house.

"But I'll get you this time!" Bubbles took off like a shot toward her sisters. With a shriek of glee, she smashed into Blossom as hard as she could. "Tag!" Bubbles yelled, crashing through the wall of the house as she tagged Blossom.

"I'll get you!" Blossom cried, laughing.

Bubbles and Buttercup sped away from the school, with Blossom right behind them.

The girls continued playing, shrieking with delight as they crashed through billboards, knocked over flagpoles, and smashed into houses throughout Townsville. They laughed with delight as they zoomed around, creating a superpowered wind that uprooted trees and sent cars flying. They were having so much fun with their new game that they didn't even notice that they were heading directly into the heart of . . . the city of Townsville!

Oh, no, girls! What are you doing? Fun is fun, but this is going too far! Stop, stop, before you destroy all of Townsville!

chapter 3

Back at Pokey Oaks Kindergarten . . .

The Professor jumped into his car. "Girls, no!" he cried. "Wait!" He took off after them.

Blossom, Bubbles, and Buttercup zoomed through Townsville. Blossom tore down a street, running at top speed. She ran so fast the street got red-hot and began to spark. Finally, it exploded into flames.

As Blossom dodged cars, Buttercup zipped through the air and turned a corner. Blossom, spotting her sister, screeched to a halt and turned around, going after Buttercup — and splitting a car right in half. Then she spotted Bubbles streaking off in the other direction. She took off after Bubbles, destroying the side of a glass building as she went.

"Whee!" Bubbles cried, flying off happily.

Blossom was gaining on her. But then Blossom came to a dead end. Where was Bubbles? Blossom looked right, then left. With a shrug, Blossom took off, tearing up the road again.

Then Blossom spotted a trail of blue light — Bubbles! The light was reflecting off a huge silver ball on the top of a skyscraper. Bubbles squinted, using her supervision. She spotted Bubbles in the distance, headed toward a subway entrance.

"Subway, huh?" Blossom said. She smiled and zoomed toward another subway entrance, scattering a huge pile of debris behind her.

Blossom flew through the subway tunnel and zoomed up the opposite stairs — appearing right in front of Bubbles!

Bubbles skidded to a stop when she saw Blossom. But she was too late.

"Tag! You're It!" Blossom said, tagging her.

Bubbles stood there for a moment, stunned. Then she crouched down and blasted off, sending rocks flying everywhere. The flying rocks smashed into nearby buildings, shattering windows and crumbling walls.

The Professor's car arrived on the scene and slid into a crater in the street. The Professor looked out the window, up into the sky.

"There they are!" he gasped.

Above him, Blossom and Buttercup were zooming around the tops of skyscrapers.

"Watch out!" Blossom called to Buttercup. "Here she comes!"

Bubbles zipped by. Blossom and Buttercup took off. Bubbles ricocheted against the silver ball at the top of the skyscraper, knocking it off the building.

As the ball bounced down to the street below, the crowd began to scream and run. The ball rolled through the city, flattening everything in its path.

Meanwhile, Bubbles continued to chase her sisters, bouncing from building to building. She zoomed and dipped, causing the street to ripple in a massive wave.

The concrete wave rolled down the street as Bubbles chased Blossom through the air. Buttercup zipped down to the street, out of her sisters' sight.

The people of Townsville continued to scream and run.

Buttercup watched her sisters and laughed. "Ha! Suckers!"

But suddenly, the wave of concrete Bubbles had caused reached Buttercup. It smacked into her and sent her into the air. A car flew up from the street alongside Buttercup and smashed through a window. Buttercup was thrown straight up into Bubbles's path.

"Tag!" Bubbles said, reaching out to touch Buttercup. "You're It!"

The Professor drove around the corner. From the driver's seat he could see the car that had flown into the air above him. It was stuck in the window of the building.

"Huh?" the Professor said.

Then the Professor spotted the girls, zooming down the street through the air high above. Quick as he could, the Professor took off after them. The silver ball from the skyscraper, which was still rolling around the city, barreled after the Professor's car.

The girls continued zooming around. Buttercup was gaining on her sisters. There was a building up ahead. Blossom and Buttercup took off in opposite directions, each flying around a different side. Buttercup looked back and forth, trying to decide. Then she took the shortest route and smashed straight through the building.

The gas tank on top of the building exploded with the impact. The people in the building screamed. But Buttercup emerged from the giant ball of fire with a big smile on her face.

"Whoa!" said Blossom and Bubbles when they saw her.

"Tag! You're It!" Buttercup yelled, tagging both her sisters at once.

"Hey!" Blossom objected. "We can't both be It!"

"Why not?" Buttercup demanded.

Bubbles reached out to Blossom. "Tag! You're It!"

"What? I can't be It twice!" Blossom said.

"Why not?" Bubbles asked.

"Okay then, tag! Now you guys are It!" Blossom said.

Buttercup reached out to Bubbles. "Tag!"

Bubbles tapped her sisters. "Tag!"

"Hey, no tag-backs!" Buttercup said.

Buttercup tagged Blossom. "Tag!"

The girls continued tagging one another, getting faster and faster. "Tag! Tag! Tag! Tag! Tag! Tag! Tag! Tag!" they yelled.

Below, the Professor pulled up in his car. He spotted the girls and gasped.

In a flash the girls took off again, chasing one another and giggling.

Meanwhile, at Townsville City Hall, in the Mayor's office . . .

The scene of destruction was clearly visible from the Mayor's own window. With an air of determination, the Mayor strode out the doors of his office and headed down the hall.

Oh, good! The Mayor's got things under control. He's going to . . . he's going to . . . well, what exactly are you going to do, Mayor?

Outside City Hall, Blossom, Bubbles, and Buttercup continued zipping through the air, smashing into everything in sight.

And below them, the worried Professor drove his car desperately through the city.

The Mayor continued his purposeful stride. His assistant, Ms. Sara Bellum, came rushing up to him.

"Mayor, Mayor!" Ms. Bellum said. "The

town is being destroyed by three girls with freakish powers."

The Mayor didn't reply, but kept walking, his gaze focused ahead.

"This is a very serious situation," Ms. Bellum continued. "Action needs to be taken immediately."

Meanwhile, in the skies above Townsville . . .
The three girls continued their game, causing destruction everywhere.

Back at City Hall, the front doors flew open as the Mayor exited the building with a powerful flourish.

That's right! Go, Mayor, go!
"Mayor? Mayor?" Ms. Bellum said.

But the Mayor kept up his determined walk. He was a man of action, a man with a plan. A man who would not stop until he had . . . *a pickle?*

The Mayor paused in front of the pickle cart

across the street from City Hall. He held up his hand for silence. He cleared his throat. "The usual," he said to the pickle vendor.

But what are those wild streaks of pink, blue, and green up above? Oh, no, it's Blossom, Bubbles, and Buttercup — and their terrible game of tag is headed this way! Watch out, Mayor!

"Yes, Mayor," the pickle vendor was saying. "I have a fine fresh vintage for you here."

"I'll take it!" the Mayor said happily, reaching for the pickle.

Meanwhile, the girls zoomed closer.

"Tag!" Buttercup cried.

"No, you're It now!" Bubbles giggled.

"Try to catch me!" Blossom taunted.

Smash! Just as the Mayor was about to take a big bite, the girls crashed right into the pickle cart. Debris and smoke were everywhere. The pickle cart was destroyed. The Mayor lay in a pool of pickle juice, surrounded by rubble.

The Professor skidded up in his car. "Girls! Girls!" he cried, hopping out.

Blossom, Bubbles, and Buttercup sat in a giant crater in the street, looking dazed.

"Girls, are you okay?" the Professor asked, kneeling down beside them.

The girls burst into giggles. "Tag, Professor!" they said gleefully. "You're It!"

Later that day!

The girls zipped around the Professor's house excitedly.

"That was fun!" Bubbles said.

"I'm so glad Mitch taught us that game!" Buttercup agreed.

"Girls," the Professor said in a serious tone. "It's almost bedtime, and I want to talk to all of you about something."

"What is it, Professor?" Bubbles asked sweetly.

"Well," the Professor began gently. "You three had a very busy day today, didn't you?"

"Yeah, it was fun," Bubbles replied. "We met lots of kids."

"And we learned things," Blossom added.

"And we played tag!" Buttercup said.

The Professor sat on the girls' bed to tuck them in. "Still, I want to talk to you about your superpowers. I'm not sure how to say this, but . . . I don't think you should use them in public anymore."

The girls looked disappointed. "Why?" they asked together.

"Your powers are very special and unique," the Professor explained. "And the people of Townsville don't really understand them yet. Unfortunately, sometimes people get scared or angry when they don't understand something special or unique."

"That's silly," Blossom said.

"I think so, too," the Professor said. "But even so, just give Townsville a little time to understand your specialness, okay?"

"We will, Professor," Blossom promised.

"Okay," Buttercup agreed.

"If you want us to, Professor," Bubbles added.

The next day at Pokey Oaks!

The Professor stopped his car in front of the school. He turned to his girls. "Okay now, girls, remember —" he began.

"Don't worry, Professor," Blossom said. "Things are going to be fine."

"Have a super-duper day, Professor!" Bubbles said.

"Bye!" Buttercup added.

The girls climbed out of the car and walked confidently into the building. But once they got inside, they saw that the classroom looked different. It was dark, and there were broken light fixtures hanging from the ceiling. Parts of the walls and the ceiling were torn open, exposing ripped wires. From every corner of the room came the sounds of hammering and sawing as workers tried to fix the damage.

"Oh, hello, girls," Ms. Keane said. "We didn't know if you'd be joining us today. Please take your seats. I have a few announcements before we start class."

The girls sat down. As soon as they did, everyone moved away from them. It was clear that no one wanted to sit with them. The kids who had treated the girls so nicely the day before were ignoring them now.

"Well, I'm sorry to say that there won't be any recess for a while," Ms. Keane announced, "because of all the repairs being done. And I'm afraid we won't have any lights or water for a while. And a broken refrigerator means that snack time is out. So, let's try to ignore all the workmen and the noise and get right to work, shall we?"

The girls looked around sadly. All the other children were glaring angrily at them now. The girls hung their heads.

Chapter 4

Meanwhile, back at the Utonium household . . .

It was time to pick the girls up from school. The Professor opened the door to get his car. But to his surprise, an angry mob had gathered outside.

"That's him!" a woman shouted. "That's the mad scientist!"

A man waved a newspaper in the air. The headline said: FREAKY BUG-EYED WEIRDO GIRLS BROKE EVERYTHING. "He's the guy who made those horrible freaks!" the man yelled.

The city of Townsville . . . was a dark and dreary city of crime.

Until Professor Utonium mixed sugar, spice, and everything nice — plus a dash of Chemical X — and created three super-powered little girls, Blossom, Bubbles, and Buttercup!

The Professor brought Blossom, Bubbles, and Buttercup to school. They liked being around all the other kids. And at recess, another kid taught them how to play a fun game — tag!

Ye Olde Townsville Crier Tribune News

BUG-EYED WEIRDO GIRLS
BROKE EVERYTHING

But the girls got so carried away with the game, they accidentally destroyed half of Townsville.

That night, the Professor told the girls they had to stop using their superpowers. The girls didn't understand why. But the next day at school, they discovered that everyone was mad at them for breaking everything.

That afternoon, the Professor didn't pick up the girls from school. So they tried to find their way home on their own. All around them were reminders of how everyone hated them now.

Blossom, Bubbles, and Buttercup got lost, and some mean Gangsters bothered them. But then they found a mysterious new friend called Jojo.

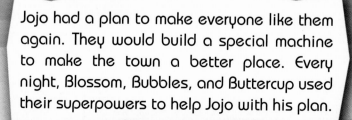

Jojo had a plan to make everyone like them again. They would build a special machine to make the town a better place. Every night, Blossom, Bubbles, and Buttercup used their superpowers to help Jojo with his plan.

When the machine was done, Mojo took the girls to the zoo to celebrate. But he had another plan in mind.... He wanted to give the monkeys at the zoo special powers, just like the girls had!

The next day, the girls brought the Professor into the city to see the great thing they had done. But Jojo had tricked them! His machine had made all the monkeys go crazy and attack the city. And now the people of Townsville hated them more than ever.

The girls were so ashamed, they flew into space to escape what they had done.

But they heard the cries of the people back in Townsville, especially the Professor, who had been kidnapped by Mojo Jojo. The girls flew back to find their father.

Then Blossom, Bubbles, and Buttercup realized they could use their powers to fight evil! The girls flew all around the city, rescuing people from Mojo's crazy monkeys.

Mojo wasn't finished yet! He drank some more Chemical X and became Mo' Mojo! But the girls were determined to defeat him — and they did!

The Mayor and the citizens of Townsville were so happy, they asked Blossom, Bubbles, and Buttercup to be their protectors. And so, for the very first time, the day was saved — thanks to The Powerpuff Girls!

"The girls who destroyed our city!" called another woman.

"That's right! He's the one!" a hysterical voice yelled as the police dragged the Professor to the jailhouse. "It's him! He destroyed my pickle cart! Bust him! Get him! Haul him in!"

"Mayor, behave!" Ms. Bellum interrupted the hysterical Mayor. She pulled out an official document and faced the Professor. "Professor Utonium, my name is Sara Bellum, Chief Deputy Assistant to the Mayor's Office. The people of Townsville are tired of the crime and destruction. And now that we have actually traced such activity back to your three children —"

"But this was just an accident!" the Professor objected. "They were just playing!"

Ms. Bellum turned to the police. "Cuff him, boys."

"But my girls!" the Professor objected. "I keep telling you, I have to go pick them up! I can't just leave them there alone! Please, please, just let me go! My girls need me!

They're waiting for me, and they don't know where I am! I told them not to use their powers, and they can't find their way if they don't fly. Please, they're only little girls!"

What, the Professor going to jail? But he never meant anybody any harm! Besides, who's going to look after the girls now?

It was a long, sad day at school for the girls. No one wanted to play with them or talk to them. Finally, it was dismissal time. The girls were more than ready to go home.

They stood outside the school building, waiting for the Professor. The minutes ticked by. But the Professor was nowhere in sight. It got later and later. The sun moved across the sky, and the shadows on the empty playground became longer.

"He's not coming," Buttercup said. "He hates us."

Bubbles started to cry.

"No, he probably just got held up," Blossom

said. "Or maybe the car broke down. Or maybe he just forgot."

They waited a while longer.

"Or maybe he does hate us," Blossom said at last. "Come on, let's try to find our way home."

Buttercup and Bubbles floated sadly into the air. But Blossom stayed on the ground.

"We're not supposed to use our powers," Blossom reminded her sisters.

"Oh, right," Buttercup said. She and Bubbles floated sadly back down to the ground.

Not at all sure of where they were going, the girls began walking.

Poor girls! All alone with no one to watch out for you! And it looks like rain, too!

Chapter 5

On the other side of Townsville, Blossom, Bubbles, and Buttercup are walking through deserted streets. It is dark and gloomy. They are tired. They are alone. And they feel . . . abandoned.

"Well, it's official," Buttercup said, looking around. "I have no idea where we are."

"I can't say this has been the best day," Blossom said.

"But it probably couldn't get much worse," Bubbles pointed out.

There was a clap of thunder, and it began to rain. Within a few minutes, it was pouring.

Buttercup snarled angrily and started to mutter.

Bubbles began to cry.

Blossom peered down a deserted alleyway. The alley was full of garbage and cartons. "Come on. Maybe there's a box we can get into for shelter," she said.

The girls headed down the alley, toward a large carton. But just as they approached it, someone leaped out of it at them!

The girls gasped.

Eeek! Who's that? Why, it's Little Arturo, of the no-good Gangreen Gang! That means that the rest of the Gang can't be far away!

One after another, four more figures jumped out of nearby boxes.

Snake! Big Billy! Ace! Grubber! Yep, the Gang's all here.

The Gangreen Gang, with their ugly green

skin and their tough-guy attitudes, were a bunch of hoodlums who enjoyed harassing Townsville's citizens for fun. And they had the girls surrounded.

Blossom, Bubbles, and Buttercup looked at the five thugs with fear.

"Awwww, what's the matter?" Ace, their leader, sneered. "Did somebody get lost?"

Big Billy, a heavyset goon with a mop of hair, let out a guffaw.

The girls looked around. They had nowhere to go. They were trapped in a dead end.

Grubber, the most horrific of the hoodlums, raised his long creepy arms in the air. He began to walk forward, closing in on the girls.

Blossom, Bubbles, and Buttercup shook with fear.

Suddenly, a flat, round object flew by and smacked Grubber in the head.

What's that? A garbage can lid? But where did that come from?

The lid continued to fly through the air like

a boomerang, spinning into Snake. Next it ricocheted off a wall and smashed down on Ace. Then it knocked Big Billy in the head. It continued on, looking like it was about to hit the ground. But then it bounced back and beaned Little Arturo right in the head.

The Gangreen Gang was down for the count. Meanwhile, the lid continued spinning and flying toward the girls until finally it was caught by an outstretched hand.

"Wow," Buttercup said. "That was cool."

The girls turned and saw the silhouette of a mysterious figure holding the lid. They stared in astonishment as the figure ran off down the alley.

"Hey, wait!" Blossom called. "Come back!"

The girls took off after the figure. They chased it through the alley, weaving among the strewn boxes.

Blossom peered into a large carton. "Hey, girls, over here!"

Bubbles and Buttercup hurried over.

The figure was huddled inside the box. "Go away," it said in a heavy, sad voice. "Please do not look at me."

"But we just wanted to thank you for saving us from those green gangsters back there," Blossom said.

"Yeah, that was amazing with the trash can lid!" Buttercup said.

"You rock!" Bubbles squeaked.

"No, please!" the huddled figure cried despairingly. "I dare not listen. For I have been lashed by harsh tongues for too long. I do not rock. For I am . . . a monster!"

"You're not a monster," Blossom said. "Monsters are evil."

"Yeah," said Buttercup, "and anybody who'd save us like you did is *soooooo* not evil."

"Please," the creature said, "you're just trying to make me feel better. But my pain is not for you to understand. How could you know what it is to be cast out into a world that only offers misery? How could you know what it is like for people to fear and despise you for the very things that make you special, because you don't fit in, because you are a . . . *freak!*" The figure jumped out at the girls, pulled off the bag covering his head, and revealed himself.

Why, it's Jojo, the jealous lab monkey with the mutated skin and brain! You don't know this, girls, but he used to live in your very own house — before Chemical X changed him. Ugh! Look at him now! His skin is greener than ever, and his brain has swollen right out of his skull!

But the girls were not scared by Jojo's appearance.

Blossom looked at the big-brained monkey. "We're freaks, too."

The girls began to float above the ground to show him what they meant.

"What amazing powers!" Jojo exclaimed.

"No! They're not amazing! They're terrible!" Blossom said.

"Everyone hates them," Buttercup explained.

"I bet everyone hates you, too," Jojo said.

"Yes," Bubbles said, her eyes filling with tears.

Jojo, too, had tears in his eyes. He turned away from the girls. "I know how you feel," he said. "This brain of mine is full of brilliant ideas. But will anyone listen to Jojo? No." He started to climb into his box.

"Don't be sad," Bubbles said. "The Professor says that sometimes people get angry when they don't understand something special or unique."

"And if you just give them time, they'll start to understand your specialness," Blossom added.

"Yeah, you just got to believe in yourself," Buttercup said.

Jojo's mouth twisted into a strange, wicked smile. "You mean, if I just take the time to construct my most ingenious plan, the . . . uh, Help-the-Town-and-Make-It-a-Better-Place

Machine, then people will come to understand my specialness?"

The girls looked at one another. They weren't so sure about this. But they really wanted to help Jojo feel better.

"Yeah, totally," Buttercup said.

"Because if you made the town better, then that would make the town . . . better!" Bubbles said.

"Then everyone would appreciate you," Blossom said.

"Okay, I'll do it!" Jojo said. He narrowed his eyes and looked at the girls. "But I will need your help. Come with me."

Oh, no, girls, don't go with him! Didn't anyone ever tell you not to go with strangers — especially strange monkeys with enlarged brains and twisted, evil smiles?

Chapter 6

Blossom, Bubbles, and Buttercup stood with Jojo on the top of the giant volcano in the center of Townsville. They stared down at the molten lava boiling below them.

"I need you to jump in there," Jojo explained. "And take this mechanical device I've built. That way we will be able to harness the energy of the earth's core for power."

"Huh?" Bubbles said.

"What?" Buttercup was confused, too.

"Why would we want to do that?" Blossom asked.

"For our plan, to make the town better, of course," Jojo replied. "Using my ideas and your powers, we will build the Help-the-Town-and-Make-It-a-Better-Place Machine. That way, everyone will see that our special abilities are good, and then everyone will love us. Remember? It was your idea."

"Oh, yeah," Blossom said doubtfully. "But use our powers?"

"No way!" Buttercup said.

"We're never using our powers again," Bubbles said.

"But your powers are great," Jojo said. "It is like you said — you just have to believe in yourselves."

The girls looked at one another, blinking. They didn't know what to do. After all, they were the ones who told him he had to believe in himself. Maybe they needed to take their own advice. They looked down at the lava. Blossom grabbed the device, and they all dove in.

Inside the volcano, the girls tunneled through the hot, fiery lava. No normal little girls could have withstood the heat. Farther and farther down they went. Finally, they reached the core and hooked up the device. Then they tunneled back to the surface.

"Yes! Yes!" Jojo cried. He jumped up and down, thrilled with their accomplishment.

"We did good?" Blossom asked.

"You did very good . . . very good indeed," Jojo replied.

"So now what are we supposed to do?" Buttercup asked.

"Go home," Jojo told them. "It will be morning soon, and you should get some rest. Each night we will meet here and do more work. But girls, you must promise me that you will not speak a word of our plan to anyone. Do you understand?"

"Not really," Blossom said.

"What's the big secret?" Buttercup asked.

"It's not a secret, it's probably a surprise!" Bubbles said excitedly.

"Uh, right!" Jojo said. "It's . . . an extra-special fun-tastical super-duperal surprise that is sooooo big that when Townsville sees it, they won't know what hit them!"

"Yay!" the girls cheered.

Thrilled with their new surprise project, Blossom, Bubbles, and Buttercup took off back home. They zoomed into the house.

"I'm so excited!" Blossom said.

"Yeah, we'll show them!" Buttercup said.

Bubbles was looking around. "Hey, where's —?"

Suddenly, the door burst open. A group of police threw the Professor in and slammed the door behind him. The Professor lay, hand-cuffed, on the floor in a heap.

"Professor!" the girls cried.

"Oh, girls," the Professor gasped. "Thank goodness you're okay."

Buttercup quickly focused her eye beams on the handcuffs, disintegrating them.

"Girls, I'm so sorry!" the Professor wailed. "You must hate me for not picking you up from school. But it's not my fault! It's this town! They've gone crazy! It's like they've never seen kids playing before. I knew your powers would take some getting used to, but jail, lawsuits, angry mobs — what's next?"

"Don't worry, Professor," Bubbles said. "Things are going to get better. We promise!"

Blossom and Buttercup turned quickly to their sister. "Sssshhhhh!"

The next night! The girls are sound asleep in their beds. But wait, no, they're not sleeping! They're wide awake! Girls, what are you up to?

The girls climbed out of bed and snuck out their bedroom door. It was late, but the Professor was still up in his office, talking on the telephone.

"Yes, Officer," the Professor was saying.

"But I can assure you that they won't be involved in any more monkey business."

Blossom, Bubbles, and Buttercup glided past the Professor's door and flew into the night. They flew over Townsville to meet Jojo.

"Hello, girls! Tonight we construct the super-structure — of our plan," Jojo explained. "But in order to do so, I need you to fly to the North Pole. There, frozen deep in the icy terrain, you will find an ancient asteroid that impacted our planet so very many centuries ago. It is comprised of powerful minerals and ores. Through a process of melting the rock into metal, we shall forge our way into Townsville's hearts. And thus build a better tomorrow!"

"Okay, Jojo," Bubbles said.

"You got it," Buttercup said.

"Anything to make the town better!" Blossom added.

Blossom, Bubbles, and Buttercup zoomed north until they reached the North Pole. They located the asteroid in the ice. Then they melted the ice with their eye beams. Buttercup slid down and grabbed the asteroid.

Blossom, Bubbles, and Buttercup flew the asteroid all the way back to Townsville and delivered it to Jojo. Then they heated it up with their eye beams and turned it into liquid metal. Next they forged sturdy beams from the special metal.

Jojo consulted his blueprints and instructed the girls on how to use the beams to build an observatory structure on top of the volcano.

Time passed. The sun began to rise. Finally, yawning, the girls flew home.

When they got in the house, they were surprised to hear that the Professor was still on the telephone. He sounded very tired.

"No!" he was saying. "I don't care if the weather bureau reports seeing three flying objects over the North Pole. I can assure you, sir, my girls were home in bed!"

chapter 7

The next night! Oh, no, girls, not again!

"Tonight you will go to the blackest depths of the Atlantic Ocean," Jojo instructed the girls. "To the iron graveyard of a fallen ship. Inside is a real sunken treasure! The electronic gadgets and goodies within will be reused and rewired — thus reviving their power and, in turn, renewing Townsville's faith in our powers."

"Okay, Jojo," Bubbles said.

"You got it," Buttercup said.

"Anything to make the town better!" Blossom added.

The girls dove into the Atlantic Ocean, and pulled up a sunken submarine. They flew the submarine back to Jojo's, where they broke it open, spilling out the electronic equipment inside.

When they returned home at dawn, they were still dripping wet. The Professor was on the phone again.

"Wrong!" the Professor was yelling. "Not true! My girls are not up to anything fishy!"

The next night!

"Tonight I need you to go to the Sahara Desert," Jojo explained to Blossom, Bubbles, and Buttercup. "Soar to the searing Sahara and stir up the sand, which we will heat until it is red-hot. Then we will forge the clearest of crystal glass for the structure, so we can make clear to the citizens of Townsville that we are to be loved, not hated."

"Okay, Jojo," Bubbles said.

"You got it," Buttercup said.

"Anything to make the town better!" Blossom added.

The girls flew to the Sahara, stirred up the sand until it was red-hot, and blew it into glass domes for the observatory.

When they returned home at dawn, the Professor was on the phone again.

"What?" the Professor was yelling into the phone. "You say they're causing tornadoes in the desert? Well, I say that's a lot of hot air!"

The next night!

"Our work is proceeding according to plan," Jojo told them. "At last, we will be accepted. At last, our greatest work is complete. Well . . . *almost* complete."

"What's wrong?" Blossom asked.

Jojo looked at the girls innocently. "Well, there is one last teeny, tiny, itsy-bitsy thing we still need. . . ." he began.

"Okay, Jojo," Bubbles said.

"You got it," Buttercup said.

"Anything to make the town better!" Blossom added.

The girls zoomed back to the house and headed for the Professor's laboratory.

The Professor was on the phone again. "Look, can't you see?" he was saying. "They're not working on some evil plan."

The girls flew into the lab. Blossom reached out and grabbed . . . *Chemical X!*

"And now, my little ones," Jojo said. "Our plans are complete." He gazed around at his observatory, which was dominated by his enormous machine. It was a huge orb with many arms sticking out of it, each leading to a separate glass container. The container of Chemical X was hooked up to the top of the great machine. Jojo smiled his twisted smile. "Yes! Yes!"

"We did good?" Blossom asked.

"You did very good, very good indeed," Jojo said.

"Now what do we do?" Buttercup asked.

Jojo stroked his chin thoughtfully. "Well, because you've done sooo good, I've got . . ."

"A surprise?" Bubbles asked eagerly.

"A special surprise!" Jojo declared.

"Yippee!" Bubbles cheered.

"What is it?" Blossom asked.

"The zoo!" Jojo said. "Today we are going to the zoo!"

The zoo? But that sounds so innocent! What are you up to, Jojo? Hmmm, whatever it is, it can't be good. . . .

Later that day at the Townsville Zoo!

Jojo followed the girls through the animal exhibits. Blossom, Bubbles, and Buttercup looked at the elephants, seals, and lions.

"This way!" Jojo demanded. He led them up a path with a sign that read PRIMATE PLAZA.

As the girls watched the monkeys, Jojo took out a camera. "Okay, girls, smile!" he said.

Blossom, Bubbles, and Buttercup lined up in front of the monkey cage.

Wait a minute! Jojo's up to something! Either that, or he's got the worst aim of any monkey photographer in the world. Why, he's not even focusing on the girls at all. He's pointing the camera at that big monkey in the cage behind them!

Jojo pressed the button on the camera. The monkey in the cage yelped.

Why, that's no camera! That's some kind of weird tracking device!

Jojo pointed his camera at another monkey, and another. Baboons, orangutans, apes, chimps — each one received a special tiny electronic dart from Jojo's camera. Finally, Jojo lowered his camera with an evil grin. "Come, girls, our work is fin — oh, I mean, time to go," he said.

"Aawww," the girls sighed. "But Jojo . . ."

"Come," Jojo said again. "Today must be over, because tomorrow is a very special day.

For tomorrow, after the sun rises, the inhabitants of this city will wake. And they will exclaim, 'Who has done this?' And then they will know that it was you three girls who did this wonderful thing for them."

Blossom, Bubbles, and Buttercup smiled proudly and followed Jojo toward the zoo's exit.

"Wow, Jojo," Bubbles said excitedly. "What will we have done?"

"Oh, something good!" Jojo exclaimed.

"Like a superefficient power source that's both inexpensive and safe for the environment?" Blossom guessed.

"Maybe," Jojo said mysteriously.

"Or a bad-vibe succulator that sucks out all the bad stuff from bad guys and stores it away forever?" Buttercup asked.

"Could be," Jojo said. "I am not saying what it is. But rest assured, tomorrow will be the dawn of a new age. Townsville will be a new place. And Townsville will be sorry — sorry for being so mean to you and to me!"

Later that night! Finally, it looks like the girls are going to get a good night's sleep. But wait! What's Jojo up to in his observatory?

Jojo sat at the controls of his new machine, laughing his evil laugh. He pressed buttons and slid levers. As he did, the tiny electronic darts in the monkeys and apes across town at the zoo were activated. The primates vanished, one by one, and reappeared inside special glass chambers in Jojo's observatory.

Once the monkeys were in place, Jojo revved up the machine. Chemical X began chugging through a tube. The gauge quivered and a red light blinked. The machine delivered Chemical X straight into the monkeys' brains. Their eyes popped open as their skin turned green and their brains began to grow.

Jojo cackled his evil laugh as he watched his army of supermonkeys come to life.

chapter 8

The next day!

First thing in the morning, the girls zipped into the Professor's office. The Professor had fallen asleep on his desk, by the phone.

"Wake up, Professor!" Buttercup said.

"Today's the big day," Blossom announced.

"Time for a surprise," Bubbles giggled.

"Huh?" the Professor said groggily.

"Today's the day when we show Townsville what our powers can really do," Blossom said proudly.

Meanwhile, in Jojo's lair . . .

Jojo suited up for his big day in a long purple cape and a helmet. He cackled evilly to himself as he looked over the row of motionless mutated monkeys in his laboratory.

Jojo strode over to a control panel and pressed a red button. The mutant monkeys began to stir and wake.

"That's right! Wake up, my brothers!" Jojo cried with glee. "It is time to show Townsville just what our powers can really do!"

Jojo headed straight toward City Hall. His army leaped wildly after him.

Meanwhile, back at the Utonium household . . .

The girls picked the Professor up and flew him toward the front door. They zoomed through the clouds with the still-sleepy Professor.

"See, we met this guy with powers like us, and everybody hated him, too," Buttercup said.

"But he had this great idea to help the town," Blossom explained.

"And make it a better place!" Bubbles piped in.

"And that way the town wouldn't hate us," Buttercup said.

"So we used our powers and his ideas," Blossom said, "to help everybody."

Meanwhile . . .

Jojo continued marching triumphantly toward City Hall. His army of monkeys was creating terror all over Townsville. People ran in the streets, screaming, as the mutant monkeys chased them.

Jojo marched up the steps of City Hall and pulled open the front doors. He marched through the halls, straight to the Mayor's office.

Jojo burst through the doors to the Mayor's office. The Mayor was sitting behind his desk.

"Clear out, man!" Jojo announced to the Mayor.

The Mayor looked startled.

Jojo picked up the Mayor and held him up to the window. Outside, the monkey army was running wild, destroying everything in sight.

"See what has befallen your city," Jojo said to the Mayor. "This is how it shall be."

Jojo carried the Mayor back down the hall. He opened the front doors of City Hall and tossed the Mayor out on the steps.

"No one can save you now," Jojo told the Mayor.

Meanwhile, in the sky, approaching Towns-ville . . .

"Wait till you see, Professor!" Bubbles said. "It's the bestest!"

"Everyone will think we rock," Buttercup said.

Suddenly they were interrupted by a loud scream from below.

"What's that?" Blossom said, stopping in midair.

The girls looked down. Below them on the street, a woman ran, screaming. Chasing her was a group of big-brained monkeys and apes.

People were screaming and running in all directions. The mutant monkeys were everywhere.

The girls flew down with the Professor for a closer look. Nearby, an ape held a car over his head, ready to throw it. A couple sat inside the car, hanging on for their lives and yelling in fear.

"This looks bad," Buttercup said.

The girls spotted Jojo on the steps of City Hall. "Jojo!" the girls called, waving.

"Blossom, Bubbles, and Buttercup! I could not have done this without you!" Jojo cried. "You mutant, bug-eyed freaks!"

The girls froze, horrified. Why was Jojo calling them that?

Meanwhile, a crowd began to surround the girls.

"It's them!" a man cried.

"They did this!" a woman yelled.

"How could you?" another woman demanded.

"Monsters!" a little boy screamed at them. The girls flew over to Jojo.

"Jojo, what's going on?" Blossom asked.

"This isn't making the town a better place," Bubbles pointed out.

"Yes it is," Jojo said. "For me." He paused and flapped open his cape with a flourish, revealing the tunic, belt, and gloves he wore underneath. He pulled out a helmet and put it on his head. "For, girls, I am no longer merely Jojo. Now, I am . . . *Mojo* Jojo!"

The girls looked at one another.

"For too long, apes and monkeys have been under the thumb of man," Mojo Jojo proclaimed. "The time has come to oppose that thumb! Now we will run Townsville!"

He raised his arms in triumph. The people of Townsville screamed in terror. The mutant monkeys of Townsville cheered with excitement.

"This is all your fault!" a woman yelled, pointing at the girls.

"No!" Blossom cried.

"We didn't mean it!" Bubbles insisted.

"This wasn't supposed to happen!" Buttercup said.

"We were trying to help!" the girls said together.

"Liars!" a woman yelled.

"Fibbers!" a man echoed.

"You've doomed us all!" another man wailed.

The girls turned to the Professor. "Please, Professor. Please believe us."

The Professor hung his head. "I don't know what to believe," he said in a low voice. "I thought you were good."

The girls gasped, stung by his words. "Nooooo!" they cried. Without glancing back, they flew away, high up into the sky.

Girls! Girls! Where are you going? Don't leave!

Chapter 9

Blossom, Bubbles, and Buttercup zoomed up, up, and away. They flew as high as they could. They flew away from Earth and burst through its atmosphere into outer space. They felt unloved, misunderstood, and unwanted.

Finally, the girls came to rest on an asteroid. Blossom sat down with a sigh of frustration. Bubbles threw herself down with a sob. And Buttercup crashed into the asteroid, thumping down angrily on its surface.

"Waaaa!" Bubbles cried.

"That jerk!" Buttercup spat out. "That big, dumb jerk! He duped us!"

"He planned it all along," Blossom said, shaking her head. "And we fell for it!"

Meanwhile, back in Townsville . . .

Mojo was standing on the steps of City Hall, grinning his evil grin.

"Yes!" Mojo Jojo said. "Now I, Mojo Jojo, have succeeded in my first, greatest, and most brilliant plan ever!" He looked around at the apes and monkeys. "And now you, my fellow simians, shall live in a world of peace, without man. And I, Mojo Jojo, shall be king!"

Suddenly, an orangutan stepped up on a car. He raised one mighty arm, and there was silence.

"You shall be king?" he said. "Preposterous! For it is I who am most suited to be ruler!" He quickly suited himself up, Mojo-style, with his own helmet, gloves, tunic, belt, and cape. "I, Ojo Tango, shall be Simian Supreme! I shall unleash the offensive omnipotence of my Orangutank!" He jumped into a giant tank and began to tear through Townsville.

Back on their asteroid, the girls sat, sulking. Buttercup started digging through the dust on the surface of the asteroid.

Bubbles looked up. "What are you doing?" she asked Buttercup.

"What does it look like I'm doing?" Buttercup said angrily. She kept digging. "I'm building a house! Because now we have to live here!"

"Live here?" Bubbles echoed.

"Yeah," Buttercup grumbled. "Don't you see?" She waved toward a hole in the dust. "This can be the bedroom . . ."

Meanwhile, back in Townsville . . .
A huge gorilla emerged from the crowd. "You and the orangutan both fail to grasp the obvious! It is I, Rocko Socko, who shall seize control and rule with an iron fist!" The gorilla

suited himself up, Mojo-style. He held up a pair of superfists of steel. Then he stomped off and began to crush the city with his fists.

Mojo was horrified. "Wait!" he cried.

Next a giant barrel came rolling down the street. A string of monkeys jumped out of the barrel and linked arms.

"Gangway! Gangway!" the monkeys cried. "For we, the Go Go Patrol, as brothers in arms, are linked to form a chain of command that will reach out and take hold of your world — and bring it tumbling down to its very foundation!"

The Go Go Patrol linked their monkey-chain up the side of a skyscraper and tore it down. Then they piled back into their barrel and rolled down the street.

"Stop!" Mojo called after them.

Then another caped and helmeted monkey burst through the crowd. "I, Hota Wata, am boiling mad! Therefore I shall unleash a scalding torrent to drown you all out."

Hota Wata strode over to the Townsville Water Dam. He blew up the dam and heated up all the water inside. Then he released torrents of the boiling water, flooding the streets.

Next a huge monkey carrying giant cymbals marched onto the scene.

"I, Cha Ching Cha Ching, symbolize chaotic calamity. Now, cower at my catastrophic cacophony!" He smashed his cymbals together. People screamed and covered their ears.

"Stop!" Mojo cried, covering his own ears.

Then a fleet of monkeys flew by overhead.

"We, the Doot Da Doot Da Doo Roos Doo Doos, shall rain on your parade!" the monkeys announced, spitting on the crowd below.

"Wait!" Mojo yelled.

A big-nosed proboscis monkey burst through the crowd, singing. "My name is Hacha Chacha, and here is my spiel," he sang. "A diabolical plan with lots of appeal! Spreading out bananas far and wide, fixing up the folks for a slippery slide!"

Hacha Chacha began to spread out banana

peels everywhere. People slipped and slid on the peels. Cars skidded off the road and crashed.

"No!" Mojo cried.

Another monkey in a helmet and cape came through the crowd.

"I, uh . . ." He paused for a moment, trying to think of a good name. "I, uh . . . Bla Bla Bla Bla, shall create a sauce of chaos, and stir up trouble, with a destructive force known as, uh . . . the tormato!"

Bla Bla Bla Bla poured some tomato sauce into a pot. He began mixing it at top speed. Soon, a tomato sauce tornado formed. The tormato whipped through the streets of the city, crashing buildings and cars.

"What?" Mojo said, watching the tormato.

Another helmeted, caped monkey came on the scene. "I, Koko Kongo . . ." he began.

He was interrupted by yet another suited-up simian, this one riding in on a giant drill. "I, Killa Drilla . . ."

Another monkey ran in, head-butting people right and left. "I, Bozo Bango . . ."

Another large monkey appeared, rolling over the streets of the city. "I, Rolo Ovo . . ."

"I, Cheata Beata . . ."

"I, Achy Breaky . . ."

"I, Smasha Crasha . . ."

"I, Cruncha Muncha . . ."

"I, Pappy Whappy . . ."

The monkeys were everywhere, announcing their evil intentions.

Meanwhile, up on the asteroid . . .

Buttercup gestured toward a rock. ". . . and this is my bed," she continued. She lay down angrily on the rock with a thud. Then she looked up at Bubbles and waved toward another rock. "That can be your bed over there."

Bubbles burst into tears again. "I don't want to sleep on a rock!" she wailed.

"Well, maybe if somebody hadn't pushed

Bubbles into the school . . ." Blossom grumbled.

"Well, maybe if somebody hadn't insisted on walking home from school," Buttercup shot back, "which ended up making us run into the biggest liar in the universe!"

"We weren't allowed to use our powers, and you know it!" Blossom cried.

"Oooh, look, it's Miss Goody-Goody!" Buttercup sneered.

"What was I supposed to do?" Blossom demanded angrily. "We weren't going to get people to stop hating us by breaking rules!"

"Oh, right," Buttercup shot back. "But it was a great idea to use our superpowers to make a so-called Help-the-Town-and-Make-It-a-Better-Place Machine!"

"I didn't see you putting up a fight!" Blossom yelled.

"Yeah, well you're gonna now!" Buttercup cried. She zoomed over to her sister and tackled her. Blossom and Buttercup began to fight, kicking up asteroid dust everywhere.

"Wait!" cried Bubbles. She cocked her head to one side, listening. "Do you hear that?"

From far, far away, the girls could hear the screams of terror from down in Townsville. . . .

Oh, girls, girls! While you argue up there in the stars, Townsville is being torn apart!

Mutant primates were taking over! Walls were crumbling, walls of water were chasing people down streets, and cars were crashing.

"No!" Mojo Jojo yelled again. "Stop! Cease! Halt! Do not continue with your ramblings! My ramblings are the ramblings to be obeyed! For I am king, supreme leader, and all-around dictator! It was I who laid the original plan and set it into motion. Don't you see that your plans are my plans because you made plans, and my plan was to make you? I am your creator, your king! I am Mojo Jojo!"

He stormed down the steps of City Hall. He stopped near the stunned Professor, who was watching the goings-on in horror. Mojo grabbed the Professor by the throat.

The Professor let out a strangled sound. "Helglp!"

Meanwhile, back in outer space . . .
"What should we do?" asked Bubbles anxiously. The screams were getting louder.

"I bet Miss Goody-Goody will say we should take responsibility for our mistakes and go help everybody," Buttercup sneered.

Blossom looked sad. Bubbles looked at her. "It sounds like they're hurting!"

Then suddenly, a faint sound began to travel toward them from the direction of Earth. The sound grew louder and louder as it got closer. It was a scream, but somehow it stood out from the other screams coming from below.

Blossom and Buttercup froze. Bubbles stopped crying.

"What's that?" Buttercup asked.

"Just somebody screaming," Bubbles said.

"That's not just somebody!" Blossom cried. "It's —"

"The Professor!" the girls shouted together. And with that, they took off like a shot.

Meanwhile, back in Townsville . . .

Suddenly, out of the night, a light burst through the sky, filling the air with pink, blue, and green streaks.

"Professor! Professor!" the girls cried, swooping down, looking for him.

Mojo was still choking the Professor. "I repeat that this is all your fault, because you made these girls! And if they had not helped me, my plan would never have been completed! And the monkeys never would have turned on me, and none of this would have ever happened! So you will pay!"

"Girls!" the Professor cried. But the girls were still flying above the rubble of Townsville, looking for him.

Oh, no! Hurry, girls, hurry!

Chapter 10

The girls flew above the mayhem, looking for the Professor. People ran in fear down on the streets below. Megabrained monkeys were storming after people, driving tanks, controlling robots, smashing walls, and crushing cars.

The Orangutank headed down a side street, shooting rockets into the air. People were running in all directions.

Bubbles spotted a woman running down the street. The woman tripped on a banana peel. Falling debris was about to crush her.

The woman screamed, "Help!!"

Out of instinct, Bubbles zoomed down to the woman and scooped her up.

"Good job, Bubbles," Blossom said. "But we've got to save —"

"That baby!" cried the woman, still in Bubbles's arms.

A baby carriage was hurtling down the middle of the street. A crazed-looking monkey was running after it.

"I'm on my way!" Blossom took off. She swooped down and grabbed the baby from the carriage just in time.

"Okay," Buttercup said, "but we still have to help —"

"That dog!" cried the woman, pointing.

A flood was carrying a dog down the street.

"I got this one!" Buttercup took off. She scooped up the dog from the water.

Bubbles set the woman down safely. "Okay, now, time for the Professor," she began.

Suddenly, there was a scream. Rocko Socko,

the gorilla with the fists of steel, had picked up a car and was about to crush it.

Another scream. Ojo Tango's Orangutank was about to smash a man in a phone booth.

"Save those people!" Blossom cried, taking off. Her sisters zoomed off behind her.

Buttercup swooped down and used her super-strength to grab the car from Rocko Socko's grip. Blossom snatched the phone booth out of the path of the Orangutank.

Suddenly, Cha Ching Cha Ching, a giant monkey with enormous cymbals, appeared. He began smashing his huge cymbals together. The force created super sound waves, breaking the windows of nearby buildings.

Now an enormous ape was stomping through town, stepping on everything in sight.

Next a whole gang of monkeys began kicking people and sending them flying.

The girls were zooming left and right, saving people as fast as they could.

"This is hopeless!" Blossom said, panting.

"There are too many monkeys!" Bubbles exclaimed.

"What can we do?" Buttercup complained. Then she turned. Rocko Socko, the gorilla with the iron fists, had grabbed the dog she had saved earlier from the water. "Get your hands off him, you darn dirty ape!"

Buttercup was furious. She couldn't stand it anymore. Before she knew what she was doing, she pulled back and — *WHAM!* Buttercup socked Rocko Socko right in the jaw. The punch sent the ape flying, slamming him into a building.

Blossom and Bubbles gasped. "Buttercup!"

Buttercup looked horrified. "I — I — I didn't mean it! It was an accident! I — I —"

Blossom stared at her sister. "Buttercup, you're a genius!"

Buttercup looked confused. "I am?"

"She is?" Bubbles asked.

"Yeah," Blossom said. "The one way to save the town and find the Professor is to use our powers to fight those monkeys!"

There was a scream from the crowd below. The Orangutank was chasing a mob of people.

"Come on!" Blossom yelled. She zipped down to the Orangutank and gave it a full-force flying kick. The Orangutank exploded into pieces.

"Wow!" Bubbles gasped.

"Let me in on some of that!" Buttercup said.

"Come on, girls," Blossom called. "Let's put an end to this gorilla warfare!"

"We're right behind you!" Bubbles and Buttercup replied.

Mojo was still choking the Professor. "I reiterate that this is all your fault, because you made these girls! And if they had not helped me, my plan would never have been completed! And the monkeys never would have turned on me, and none of this would have ever happened! So you will pay!"

"Girls!" the Professor cried again. He could see them streaking around the city, saving people. But the girls were so busy fighting crazed monkeys, they didn't hear him.

Mojo covered the Professor's mouth. "Shut up! I was afraid of this. They have returned and found out just what their powers can really do. Come! You will make a good power-proof vest." Mojo picked up the Professor and took off with him.

Meanwhile, Cha Ching Cha Ching was slamming his cymbals together, creating vibrations like an earthquake. Buttercup flew in and kicked him in the head. Blossom followed, socking him in the gut. Finally, Bubbles punched him in the jaw, sending him flying.

The girls saw the flood rushing through the streets below. Hota Wata, the monkey who had broken the dam, was riding a giant wave.

The girls zoomed toward the street, creating a hole as a drain. The water flowed into the hole, taking Hota Wata down with it.

A giant barrel rolled into view. The barrel popped open and a string of monkeys jumped out, linking arms.

Buttercup grabbed the arm of one monkey and jerked him like a whip, sending a vicious wave through his pals. Blossom took hold of another monkey and pulled the line up as tight as she could. Then Blossom let them go, sending them flying. Bubbles caught the line of monkeys and began skipping rope, whacking them hard on the ground at each turn.

"Wheee!" Bubbles said, her blond pigtails flying. "This is fun!"

There were monkeys raining down all around the girls. But none of them had the Professor.

Blossom turned to her sisters. "Come on, girls. We've got one more bit of monkey business to take care of."

Together, Blossom, Bubbles, and Buttercup took off, sending streaks of pink, blue, and green across the sky. They sped toward Mojo Jojo's lair and smashed through the doors.

"Not so fast, Mojo Jojo!" the girls yelled.

Mojo Jojo sneered at them. He held the Professor by the arm. "Ah, yes, look!" he said. "The little heroes have come to save Daddy!"

"No, girls!" the Professor cried. "Forget me! Save yourselves!"

Mojo tightened his grip on the Professor, twisting his arm. The Professor gasped in pain.

"Don't hurt him!" Bubbles said.

Mojo Jojo let out a maniacal laugh. "If you'll excuse me, I, Mojo Jojo, have a town to take over. I have a world to rule. I have to seize control of an area and force its inhabitants to follow my way of thinking."

Mojo made his way over to his control panel, still dragging the wincing Professor with him. Mojo pulled levers and pressed buttons. The machine began to hum and beep.

"Even if it means taking *X-treme* measures," Mojo added.

The girls looked up at the container of Chemical X. Mojo stuck the plug from the machine directly into his helmet. The Chemical X began draining into Mojo's brain.

The girls gasped.

The machine began humming louder, beeping faster. Lights on the panel were flashing.

The Chemical X poured into Mojo Jojo's brain faster and faster. His brain began to bulge out of his helmet. His eyes bugged out of his head. His body swelled.

As Mojo's body ballooned, he dropped the Professor. The girls flew over and scooped him up. Mojo's swelling body burst through the walls of the observatory. Bricks and glass and pieces of wall flew everywhere.

"Now I am even *mo'* Mojo than befo'!" the giant Mojo roared. With a mad gleam in his eyes, he leaped down from the volcano and stomped toward the city.

Mo' Mojo Jojo? Wasn't he Mojo enough?! Somebody's got to stop this pumped-up primate!

Chapter 11

Blossom, Bubbles, and Buttercup climbed out from under the observatory debris. They pulled the Professor out with them.

"Girls!" the Professor cried. "Thank goodness you're okay! Now, let's get out of this town and find a safe place to live."

Buttercup shook her head. "It's no use, Professor."

"We already tried running away," Blossom explained. "Now we have to help fix the problem we helped start."

"You said to give everyone a little time to understand our specialness," Bubbles reminded him. "Well, now it's time for everyone to understand!"

"Especially Mo' Mojo!" the girls said together.

The girls zoomed off into the air, leaving the Professor with a proud smile on his face.

Mo' Mojo was stomping toward City Hall. The ground there was still littered with defeated and beaten monkeys and apes.

"Now!" Mo' Mojo roared. "As I was saying before I was so rudely interrupted by your meaningless monkeyshines, I, Mojo Jojo, have succeeded in my first, greatest, and most brilliant plan ever!"

In one sweep, Mo' Mojo ripped off the dome of City Hall. He put the round cap of the building on his head like a crown. "Now I, Mojo Jojo, shall be king!"

Then giant Mojo Jojo felt three sharp pings in his side. He teetered and almost lost his balance.

"Surrender now, and we'll go easy on you!" a chorus of tiny voices shouted.

Mo' Mojo looked around.

"Down here!" the voices yelled.

Mo' Mojo looked down. Way down. He spotted Blossom, Bubbles, and Buttercup standing by his left foot.

"Oh, isn't that cute?" Mo' Mojo said. "You are actually trying to stop me!" He laughed.

"*Trying?*" Bubbles said.

"We *will* stop you!" Blossom countered.

"Who are you calling *cute?*" Buttercup demanded.

"Okay, let's play!" Mo' Mojo reached down and tried to squash the girls. But they shot out from underneath his giant hand. Bubbles hit him on the nose with a streetlight. The girls leaped, whizzed, and flew around Mo' Mojo, making him flail about wildly. Blossom and Bubbles came in on either side of his face and slammed him. Buttercup flew up and kicked

Mo' Mojo hard in the backside, sending him up into the air. The sight was so funny, Buttercup burst out laughing.

Mo' Mojo glared angrily. He took one step forward toward Buttercup — and stepped on her.

"Buttercup!" Blossom yelled.

Blossom and Bubbles stopped in midair, staring in horror at Mo' Mojo's foot. Having caught them off-guard, Mo' Mojo gave both girls a monkey-punch, sending them flying through the air and into a building.

But then Buttercup pulled herself out from under Mojo's giant foot. She socked him, giving him a super stubbed toe.

"Yow!" Mo' Mojo hopped up and down on one foot in pain.

Blossom and Bubbles emerged from the building, zooming straight into Mo' Mojo's middle. *POW!* Mo' Mojo flew back from the force.

"Good job, girls!" Blossom said.

But Mo' Mojo came staggering back. He reached out and grabbed Blossom and Buttercup, squeezing them tight.

Bubbles flew in to attack. She shot her eye beams at him, searing the monkey fur across his chest. Mojo winced in pain, releasing Blossom and Buttercup.

The three girls buzzed around Mo' Mojo. He swatted wildly at them, knocking them to the ground. Then he scooped them up in his hands. He brought them to his giant green face.

"Fools!" Mo' Mojo said. "You dare to challenge me? You attempt to defeat me? I, Mojo Jojo, who saved you, who took you in, who befriended you, who taught you the boundless limits of your powers?"

Mo' Mojo stormed through the city. He climbed up a skyscraper, with the girls still tight in his hands. The girls wriggled, trying to get free.

Mo' Mojo held the girls out over the city. "Can't you see? The people of Townsville will never understand you as I can. For we are kindred spirits, whose powers spring from the same source."

"Never!" Blossom blurted out. "We're not the same as you!"

"No!" Mo' Mojo said. "We are the same! We are not like them! For we are stronger! We are invincible! We have the power! And we shall rule! Don't make me destroy you! Join me, girls, join me!"

"Nooo!" the girls cried together.

Buttercup began to concentrate, a determined look on her face. Blossom and Bubbles did the same. Together, they mustered every bit of power they had. In a huge burst of energy, they broke free from Mo' Mojo's grip.

The girls shot up and away from Mo' Mojo. He looked at them angrily, his giant hand still smoking from their blast.

Blossom zoomed in and socked Mo' Mojo in the face. He began to lose his balance and grabbed onto the skyscraper's spire. "We'd

never join you and it's because we're stronger!"
she cried.

Bubbles flew toward Mojo and kicked him.
"Because we are invincible!"

Buttercup swooped around and socked him
in the jaw. "Because we have the power!"

Mo' Mojo was reeling, losing his grip. The
girls continued buzzing around him. Bubbles
gave him a punch. Buttercup gave him a whack.
Blossom gave him a crack.

"That we have to protect them from you!"
the girls cried together.

"It's you who is to be feared!" Blossom declared.

"'Cause you are a monster!" Bubbles yelled,
kicking Mo' Mojo's helmet.

"You are evil!" hollered Buttercup, bashing
him in the face.

Mo' Mojo was barely hanging on. The three
girls swooped around and came straight at
him. They stopped right in front of his face.

"And you are 'It'!" they yelled as one. They

tagged Mo' Mojo, pushing him backward. He lost his balance and tumbled through the air.

A voice called up from the street below. "Girls!"

"It's the Professor!" Bubbles said.

"And Mojo's falling straight toward him!" Buttercup said.

"Come on, we have to save him!" Blossom declared.

The girls zoomed into action. The Professor was on the ground, holding a vial of red liquid. The girls swooped down and picked him up. But as they grabbed him, the Professor lost his grip on the vial.

"Oh, no!" the Professor said. "I dropped the Antidote X!"

"Antidote X?" Blossom said.

Just then, Mojo came crashing down, landing smack dab on the vial of red liquid. A red puddle began to leak out from under him.

"It's an antidote to Chemical X," the Professor explained quickly. "I just whipped some up."

The girls watched as Mojo Jojo began to shrink back down to size. The puddle of Antidote X oozed around him.

The Professor turned to the girls. "Oh, girls, I'm so sorry for doubting you. You are good, good, perfect, perfect little girls, and I love you!"

"We love you, too," the girls said together.

"And we're really sorry," Blossom said.

"We messed up," Buttercup said.

"But we're ready, Professor," Bubbles said solemnly.

The girls flew slowly toward where Mojo was lying in the red puddle.

"Ready?" the Professor asked, confused. "For what?"

"To take the Antidote X to get rid of our powers," Blossom said.

"If it wasn't for them, none of this would have happened," Bubbles said.

"Everyone will probably stop hating us if we're just normal," Buttercup said.

Suddenly, from behind the girls, there was a chorus of "No! No! No!"

The girls whipped around. A crowd of Townsville's citizens had gathered. At the head of the crowd were the Mayor and Ms. Bellum.

"Um, well, uh, don't do that," the Mayor stammered. "You see, that was pretty good, what you did . . . with the flying . . . and the punching . . ."

Ms. Bellum stepped forward. "I think what the Mayor is trying to say is, we're sorry, and thank you, girls."

Ms. Keane stepped out of the crowd. "Girls, that was wonderful, just wonderful," she said, beaming.

"Amazing!" a man added.

"Thanks!" Talking Dog declared.

The girls broke into huge smiles.

The Mayor stepped forward. "You know, girls, this town really stinks. So I was wondering, uh . . ." He looked down shyly at his feet.

"Well . . . uh, could we maybe sometimes call you girls to save the day or something?"

"Can we, Professor?" the girls asked excitedly.

"Hmmm," the Professor said, thinking. There was a twinkle in his eye. "Well, I don't know. I guess that would be okay, as long as it's before your bedtime."

"Yay!" the girls cheered. They zoomed up into the air.

The crowd cheered. The Mayor beamed.

Sugar, spice, and everything nice. Those were the ingredients chosen to create the perfect little girl. But Professor Utonium accidentally added an extra ingredient to the concoction . . . Chemical X! Thus, Blossom, Bubbles, and Buttercup were born! Using their ultra superpowers, they have dedicated their lives to fighting crime and the forces of evil!

And so, for the very first time, the day was saved, thanks to The Powerpuff Girls!